As for little Bella, she worried a lot.
So Daddy called her Little Baby Not-Sure.

One winter morning Daddy said,
"Who wants to go ice-skating today?
The lake is frozen hard!"

"Me, me, me!"
said Ben.

"Me, me, me!"
said Sophie.

But Bella was worried about skating.
What if she looked silly and everyone laughed at her?
"I'm not sure," she said.

"Don't worry, Little Baby Not-Sure," said Daddy.
"Eat a good breakfast, and then you'll be ready
for skating."

"I'm having *two* smoothies for breakfast," said Ben. "I'm a speedy eater!"

"Well done, Big Brother Rushabout!" said Daddy.

Sophie ate up all her fruit and yogurt without spilling one bit.

"Well done, Big Sister Tidypaws!" said Daddy.

But Bella just played with her porridge, and she wouldn't
eat the rest of her breakfast. She still wasn't sure about
skating. She only had little legs. What if she couldn't keep up?

Right after breakfast Daddy said,
"Come on, little rabbits! Let's get ready
to go out."

"I'm the fastest!" said Ben.

"Well done, Big Brother
Rushabout!" said Daddy.

"And I look the neatest!" said Sophie.

"That's right, Big Sister Tidypaws!"
said Daddy.

But Bella wouldn't put on her hat and scarf.

She still wasn't sure about skating.
What if she fell over and hurt herself?

So Daddy said, "Don't worry, Little Baby Not-Sure.
Let's just have some fun in the snow first."

"Yes! Let's all make a snow rabbit!" shouted
Ben and Sophie.

So Bella went outside with the others.
But instead of making a snow rabbit . . .

. . . she made a snow mouse!
That made everybody laugh.

"Well done, my Funny Bunny!"
said Daddy.

Then Ben and Sophie wanted to go sledding.

"Good idea!" said Daddy. "All aboard!"

And before Bella had time to start worrying,
off they went, sliding over the snow.

Soon they were rushing down the hill with the wind whooshing in their ears. But suddenly they came to a bumpy bit.

Up in the air went Ben and Sophie.

And down they went—plop—into a snowdrift!

But Bella held on tight all the way to the bottom. *She* didn't fall off at all!

"Well done, my Slippy Slider!" said Daddy, laughing.

They stopped at the edge of the lake, and Daddy said, "Skates on, everyone!"

But Bella was worried again.

What a VERY BIG lake it was!
And what a lot of skaters!

So Bella just sat and watched with Daddy.
Then she said, "Look at that funny bunny! I was a
funny bunny when I made my snow mouse, wasn't I?"

"Yes, you were!" said Daddy.

"And look at that slippy slider!
I was a slippy slider when I stayed
on the sled, wasn't I?"

"You were the *best* Slippy Slider!"
said Daddy.

That made Bella feel a lot
more sure of herself.
"Maybe I can be a
skater, too!" she said.

So she laced up her skates,

and one paw . . .

two paws . . .

she stepped onto the ice!

And she went **SSSSSlip!**

She went **SSSSSSlide!**

And suddenly . . . Bella was skating!

"This is FUN!" she shouted.

"Well done, Bella!" called Daddy.

"You're a super skater!" said Ben and Sophie.

After the skating was over, Daddy said
they could all have hot chocolate.

So Ben ran and fetched some extra-quick!

"Well done, Big Brother Rushabout!"
said Daddy.

Sophie did the pouring,
and she didn't spill a drop.

"Well done, Big Sister Tidypaws!"
said Daddy.

Bella drank a great big mugful
and said it was the BEST EVER.

"Well done, my little
Super Skater!" said Daddy.

And as they walked home,
Daddy said, "Wasn't skating fun today?
Who wants to go again tomorrow?"

"Me, me, me!" said Ben.

"Me, me, me!" said Sophie.

But Bella said, "I'm not sure . . ."

"Not sure about skating?" asked Daddy.

"No! I'm not sure I can wait till tomorrow!"
shouted Bella.

"Three cheers for Bella!"
said Ben and Sophie.

"Hip hip hooray!" said Daddy.

And do you know, he never called her Little Baby Not-Sure ever again!